UKIYO

Stories of "The Floating World"
of postwar Japan

Selected and edited by
JAY GLUCK

The Vanguard Press, Inc., New York

To

PAUL YOSHIRO SAEKI, O.B.E.

*on his 92nd birthday
and 75 years of "interpretation"
teacher and friend*

ACKNOWLEDGMENTS

The Imperial Rescript on Surrender is from *The Nippon Times* (now *Japan Times*) of August 15, 1945 (courtesy of Ogata Tamotsu).

The following translations appeared in the original Orient edition of *Ukiyo* (Phoenix Books, Tokyo, 1954), copyright 1954 by the editor and publisher, Jay Gluck: *Revenge* by Mishima Yukio, **Love in the Annam Jungle* by Oka Masamichi, †* *Black Out* by Koyama Itoko, *The Communist* by Abe Tomoji, *Black Market Blues* by Koh Haruto, *Ups and Downs* by Shibaki Yoshiko, †*The Only One* by Nakamoto Takako, †*Rice Weevils* by Wada Den, *Sazanka by Kawachi Sensuke, *One World by Serizawa Kojiro. (Those marked * appeared by arrangement in *Orient Digests;* those marked † in *Preview,* Tokyo.)

Appearing originally in *Preview* and reprinted by arrangement with the publisher: *Three Unforgettable Letters* by Taguchi Shu, *Captured by Americans* by Fuji Seii.

Appearing originally in, and copyright 1955 by, *Orient Digests*, Tokyo, reprinted by arrangement with the publisher: *The Admiral That Davy Jones Didn't Want* by Yokoi Toshiyuki, *Homecoming 1945* by Akiyama Isa, *These Ten Years* by Kon Hidemi, *Please Not a Word To Anybody* by Mizuki Yoko, *A Date* by Saisho Foumy, *Bringing Up Mothers-in-Law* by John Fujii.

Underground Escape from the book of the same name by Tsuji Masanobu, copyright 1951, and *Damoi—Homeward Bound* from *Four Years in Hell* by Yamamoto Tomomi, copyright 1952 by Asian Publishing, Tokyo, reprinted by arrangement with the publisher.

The Affair of the Arabesque Inlay by Ishikawa Tatsuzo appears in translation by prior arrangement through *Orient Digests*.

The Sad Samurai from *Tears on the Tatami* by John Fujii, copyright 1954 by Phoenix Books, Tokyo (Jay Gluck).

Banshu Plain by Miyamoto Yuriko appears in translation by arrangement with the author's widower, Mr. Moyamoto Kenji.

The Crane That Cannot Come Back by Seto Nanako, copyright 1961 by The Committee for the Book, Hiroshima YMCA, reprinted by arrangement with The Committee.

Echoes from a Mountain School by Eguchi Koichi reprinted through the courtesy of UNESCO.

Portions of the *Introduction* appeared by subsidiary arrangement in *Thought,* Delhi, India, 1962.

TRANSLATIONS:

JAY GLUCK: *Captured by Americans.*

GRACE SUZUKI and JAY GLUCK: *Revenge, Love in the Annam Jungle, Black Out, Black Market Blues, Please Not a Word To Anybody, Ups and Downs, The Only One, Rice Weevils, Sazanka, The Communist, One World.*

MOMOI MAKOTO and JAY GLUCK: *The Admiral That Davy Jones Didn't Want, These Ten Years, The Affair of the Arabesque Inlay.*

SAKAGUCHI YUKIKO and JAY GLUCK: *Banshu Plain.*

HASHIZUME SUMIKO: *A Crane That Cannot Come Back.*

KIMURA MICHIKO and GENEVIEVE CAULFIELD: *Echoes From a Mountain School.*

AKIYAMA ISA (author): *Homecoming 1945.*

YAMAMOTO TOMOMI (author): *Damoi—Homeward Bound.*

Preview staff (Jay Gluck, editor): *Underground Escape.*

Three Unforgettable Letters, The Sad Samurai, A Date, and *Bringing Up Mothers-In-Law* were originally written in English.

CONTENTS

———————————

INTRODUCTION

At the court of an emperor (he lived it matters not when) there was, among the many gentle arts, one which though not of very high rank was favored far beyond all the rest; as a result, the great looked with scorn and hatred upon the upstart. Thus, preponderant though it was, it was soon worn out with petty vexation, fell into a decline, and grew melancholy and retiring.

The Occidental arriving in Japan will often feign a Japanese-ness by studying the tea ceremony or sleeping on the floor alongside a perfectly good bed or decking himself out in an ill-fitting kimono, secondhand and at least a decade out of style. Not wishing to go against time-hallowed custom, I open my maiden anthology with a paraphrase of the opening lines of what is probably the world's first real novel, and certainly the greatest classic of Japanese literature, *The Tale of Genji* (11th century). This invocation of an older and greater work was a favorite Japanese literary technique, although it is now even more out of fashion than the kimonos my tourist friends take home; however, this in no way detracts from their beauty or their practicality, or from the fact that novelist Lady Murasaki, by means of this technique, presents a concise history of a thousand years of Japanese fiction.

The Japanese word *sho-setsu* is usually translated as "novel." However, the literal meaning is "small view," implying a narration of a life, or an account of living, which will take less time to read than to live through, and which might run, as *Genji,* some three-quarters of a million words or, as some in this selection, a few hundred. The English term "novel" implies, according to Webster, "a compact plot and a point." The Japanese *sho-setsu* may very well have this, but it more than likely will not. The common Occidental understanding of the Oriental attitude that this phenomenal existence called life has no logical plot, and possibly no point to it either, should make further explanation unnecessary—just as the fact that some stories *do* have a plot, even a compact one, and *do* make or come to or have a point, should show that this Oriental attitude is not so simply stated and perhaps not so universally accepted. The *sho-setsu,* then, encompasses the whole of prose fiction. We should not expect it to conform to our standards or to our ideas or definitions. It is compartmented, perhaps more so than our own, but not always in the way ours is. This should only point out to us the utter arbitrariness of any such divisions.

The "gentle arts" are at least as numerous and probably more varied in Japan as anywhere else, and among them fiction has been "not of very high rank." Certainly that of highest rank has been the dance. It is an essential element in all of the Japanese performing arts, from pure dance, both sacred and (at one extreme) very profane, through the various forms of dance-drama, which also run the gamut from the sacred to the most profane; the combat dances, from spectator sports like sumo-wrestling (whose performers are called literally wrestle-dancers), to the dance calisthenics of judo, karate, and various armament drills; the etiquette dances which ritualize the making of tea, the reception at court or in a private home, the offerings to deity, the geisha's serving her client, the artist's warming-up rituals, and even that choreography of the artist's brush known as calligraphy. Like the plastic arts, the graphic arts have, in Japan as elsewhere, enjoyed "high rank" and imperial and noble patronage.

In literature Japan has differed little from other cultures in bestowing high rank on poetry and dialectics, the oldest recorded literature being a sanctified official history and an anthology of the poetry of emperors, nobles, and commoners. Both types were compiled by imperial command.

In *The Tale of Genji* the hero discusses with the heroine the romances and popular literature. (Popular, that is, with those who could read—a limited though larger group than 11th century Europe presented.) He questions whether these are good things for a young girl to read; he questions their relation to life—or the good life. This discussion indicates that these romances and the diaries, which we might term confession stories, were "looked upon with scorn" and read in the privacy of the bedroom—but "favored far beyond all the rest" of the literary and art forms in being so widely read and appreciated. Little of the poetry and certainly none of the religious or pseudo-religious and statist dialectics ever enjoyed such popularity. Prose fiction, then, enjoys a world-wide acceptance as being that which one takes to bed to read for other than its purely soporific qualities. Persians and Indians give equal recognition to their long poems, novels in rhyme; but Japanese literature has none. Even twelve centuries ago when Japanese tastes in poetry were broader and poems were of greater stylistic variety and length, a few minutes was enough to read one through. Perhaps the language is too staccato in structure; a long poem might rattle its characters and readers apart; or perhaps the same quality makes much of the prose poetic enough. A European can take his playwrights to bed with him, but most of the best Japanese theatrical literature is better not separated from its spectacle and dance and cacophonous instrumental accompaniment. A Christian or Jew might take his Scripture to bed; the Japanese has spared himself the sanctification of his best old literature. But lives there a literate anywhere who does not take a novel of romance or adventure into his most private apartment?

The Japanese write in a script which is a mixture of the Chinese ideographs and their own syllabary, the former used singly or in combination for the root of a word, with the latter indicating the verb ending, adjective or adverb suffixes, and the like. Thus the verb "eat" might be written with a character "X," so that "eaten" would be X-en, "eating" would be X-ing. To complicate matters, X alone might be read as eat, ate, food, cuisine, depending upon context; each ideograph having at least two readings, one Japanese and one a distorted Chinese, and often four or five. There are about 45,000 of these ideographs, but modern Japanese use but a fraction of these. The newspapers and popular magazines limit themselves to fewer than 2,000, expressing more complicated words in the purely phonetic syllabary. Foreign loan words, of which English is said to have provided some 7,000, mostly technical, are almost always written in the syllabary. Again, there are two dissimilar syllabaries, with two symbols for each syllable: thus a-i-u-e-o, ka-ki-ku-ke-ko, etc., for other consonant-vowel syllables. One of these is a square-shaped series used today mostly for foreign words, or on printed signs, much as we would use a square, easy-to-read, Roman lettering. The other is a lovely flowing style, preferred by Lady Murasaki and used today for the root endings and native words not written in ideographs. As complicated as this sounds, it is a generalization and simplification of the actual state of affairs. Even the syllabary has odd readings and exceptions to its rules almost as maddening as English spelling.

The Chinese have been writing in some form for at least 4,000 years. The script was developed to about what it is today perhaps 800 years before Christ. Confucius and Lao-Tse used it over 2,500 years ago. The script was introduced into Japan by hired Korean scribes perhaps a few centuries after Christ, but the Japanese didn't really catch on to the concept of it until about the middle of the sixth century A.D. And then, as they have done so many times, they exploded into action. The emperor ordered the legends and annals of the imperial clan, and some of those of others which did not conflict too much, to be recorded. The *Kojiki* was produced in 712, and the *Nihongi* in 720, by taking down records which until then had been preserved orally by official memorizers. But the Japanese and Chinese languages bear no relation to each other and it was found to be easier to write in Chinese than to attempt to adapt the Chinese script to the spoken Japanese language. An anthology of some 4,500 Japanese poems by 450 different poets, the *Manyoshu,* or Myriad Leaves, was compiled and recorded about 760 A.D. (A selection of 1,000 were superbly translated and published in Tokyo in 1940, and the scholar-poet Ken Yasuda has published other excellent samplings since the war.) The *Manyoshu* poems use the sound values of the Chinese characters to record the sounds of the Japanese words, in effect an intricate rebus writing. Imagine an Englishman writing in pictures using fractured French pronunciation: draw an eye, French *oeil,* and here indicating the English word "we"; or two eyes, *yeux,* for "you."

Soon the two syllabaries were developed by abbreviating certain ideographs beyond recognition and using them to indicate sounds only (much as our own alphabet evolved, "A" being an abbreviated picture of an ox, called Aleph, etc.). Chinese loan words came into the language along with the writing system, as well as an alternate Chinese way of pronouncing each ideograph. They were used grammatically as Japanese, with verb endings, in Japanese word order, and often with somewhat changed meaning. The language developed a great mystique and few could learn to write it—which pleased the ruling elite. But practical women of the educated class simplified matters, writing in the everyday speech and using the sound characters, the syllabary, almost exclusively. Personal diaries were kept in this way, romantic tales were jotted down, and the literature of fiction was born.

Most of the early novelists and romantic diarists were women of the educated court class, of whom the greatest was, of course, Murasaki Shikibu, Lady Purple, authoress of *The Tale of Genji*. The 13th to 17th centuries were marked by the Mongol invasions and internal wars, to which vassal lords brought combat artists and war correspondents to record their valor for posterity and to document their claims for expenses and a share of the spoils from their liege lords. A parallel development was the war tale, which became more fictitious as time went on. *The Heike Story* is a modern chop-suey version of one of the greatest of these, and is available in English. The old diary styles continued, now written by men, often sage recluses, as the *Hojoki* (Jottings from My Ten-foot-square Hut), of about 1212 A.D., and the *Tsurezuregusa* (Harvest of Leisure), about 1330. Both are available in English, the latter in paperback. At this time the Noh-drama developed from old folk plays and Buddhist miracle plays interpreted in Zen style. The best are by a father and son, Kannami and Zeami (active from 1370 to 1443). From these, readapted for a merchant and plebeian audience and livened up in a snappy review style, evolved the Kabuki plays of the 17th and later centuries.

Japan closed herself off from the world in 1637. During the following period the flamboyant Kabuki developed; poetry thrived as ever, but mostly limited to the short epigrammatical forms which had predominated in the *Manyoshu*. Confucianism was rediscovered with a vengeance, and endless dialectic tracts and commentaries and critiques were turned out (the most important of which monopolize the English-language collection misnamed *Sources of the Japanese Tradition*), as well as popular colloquial Buddhist commentaries. But more important was the boom in books meant to entertain.

Cheap printing from carved woodblocks had been introduced into Japan along with writing back in the 6th century. It was first used for reproducing Buddhist sutras. Now the technique was turned to producing the novels once laboriously hand-scripted. Competition

increased as the publishers and writers multiplied faster than the
newly and rapidly developing plebeian literate class. Prices came
down and cheap paperbacks were ground out. To increase sales
appeal, illustrators were hired, color techniques developed, and the
ukiyo-e prints, the famed Japanese woodblock prints, blossomed as a
great art in itself. These cheap novels were about the lives of the
type of people who read them: gay blades of the city, shrewd mer-
chants, professional women, actors and artists. They are a running
commentary on the city life of that gay Floating World, the *Ukiyo*,
as it called itself from a Chinese poem. They are living, poignant,
humorous, written in the snappy, slangy speech of the time (and
sometimes untranslatable even by Japanese scholars). The best sam-
pling of two of the best writers' works is Howard Hibbett's superb
The Floating World in Japanese Fiction. These are often short
stories, which appeared in series, comprising an over-all long novel.
The important aspect of these stories, as relating to our modern
Japanese writers, is that these men wrote in concise language, rather
than the painfully indirect, abstruse, verbose, erudite styles of the
dialecticians of the "official" literature. From this tradition comes
the modern Japanese newspaper style, and it almost certainly influences some of the seemingly Western modern writers.

In 1853 Commodore Perry appeared and demanded that Japan
end her seclusion. By 1867 she had done so, again with a vengeance.
Western literature was translated helter-skelter. The old-style cheap
paperbacks went the way of similar booms in the West, getting
cheaper and appealing to lower tastes. The men of vision and edu-
cation were now learning Western languages in the new colleges,
absorbing Western ways, translating Western literature (and pap),
and very consciously affecting Western style in their own writing.
But with these many "petty vexations" literature "fell into a decline, growing more melancholy and retiring." The inability of the
new ways to produce quick solutions to Japan's problems, along
with a resurgence of those who wished to transform and readapt
the old ways, brought on a clash between liberals with no tradition
to bolster them and new samurai with an imported Prussian mili-
tarism grafted onto the old traditional warrior roots. The writers,
melancholy beyond reprieve, retired. As the novelist-critic Takami
Jun noted, in a recent PEN club talk, Japanese literature of the
past fifty years has been a hermit's literature.

The literary archaeologist-anthologist is prone to reconstruct an evolutionary chart, a family tree, in terms of his own experience. He would build or reconstruct the ruin of a paradise garden in the image of a shard of a willowware plate. He would clutter the world with *chinoiserie,* toast his world in Delft, a technique that is, of course, reciprocated—for exchange is a two-way street. What Western visitor to Japan has not looked with—what . . . a mixture of horror or shock, amusement or trepidation—upon some Japanese attempts at reproducing a specific style of Western building? (But I am prejudiced, working from my own Japanese experience, having lived here in a typical example of Japanese Ameriquasirie, a none-such version of Bible-belt barn architecture.)

Any anthropologist knows how dangerous yet essential it is to question a native informant. Ask an aborigine, "Who is your sire?" and he may point to the man who shot his totemic animal about the time his mother got her pains, or he may point to his mother's brother, or, just possibly, the gentleman who made a habit of sleeping with mom. His concept of relation, of family, will not necessarily be yours. To the Japanese the spiritual continuity of the family name is more important than blood (which may be thicker than water, but ink with which the family records are written is thicker yet). The great art and culture dynasties are maintained not by childbirth but by adoption. In Kyoto I was introduced to the "family" from which a great lady from an ancient art family had reputedly come. There was no resemblance between daughter and "parent" beyond the superficial similarities of class. I learned later that she had risen from quite low estate through her ability, and had been chosen as a bride (by a family committee) to infuse new blood into the line. To give her a proper ancestry, she was adopted out to a good family in another city (who could use the forthcoming contractual link), then brought back to Kyoto as a "bride from a fine old family." Another time I was admonished by a Japanese friend who was afraid that my interest in a certain noted geisha was too serious and would jeopardize my future aspirations, yet she was his own natural half-sister. (To keep her as a hobby, of course, would have been helpful to such aspirations.)

Literature reflects a culture's soul. It is but one of several media by which culture expresses itself in the phenomenal world. If a literature is to reflect such a seemingly casual, yet ritualized, arbi-

trariness of approach to the product of sleeping on the floor, how
are we to appreciate it from our padded pedestals? Roll off onto the
floor and "ask an informant"?

"Japanese artist, from whence comest thou?"

"I am from Kyoto, the Paris of Japan" (or if he's America-
oriented, ". . . the Boston of Japan," or ". . . the Florence of
Japan," and I once heard a Japanese travel-writer disputing with
an archaeologist, before a Persian guest, whether to compare Kyoto
with Isfahan or Shiraz). Artists are similarly compared. A Japanese
painter acclaimed as the van Gogh of Japan saw his first van Gogh
when his public-relations-expert–manager posed him before one.
One of the recent and last, supposedly, ukiyo-e artists of the old
school is officially listed as heir to a great dynastic name, implying
inheritance of a specific dynastic style. His accession to the position
was based on convenience; he had not studied with any predecessor
and in fact worked for the most part in Occidental watercolors, in
Occidental proportion and perspective—and could not even claim
to have been influenced by any of the French impressionists whom
his own dynastic forebears had influenced. The work of another
present-day Japanese painter, a disciple of Matisse, bore no resemblance to that of his master except in the coloration, and that, in
truth, was the only aspect of his art heritage he had retained.

Among Japanese writers, one drew acclaim from his American
publisher: "Proust, a Japanese Proust. . . ." And when asked what
he thought of Proust, replied, "Who is he?" Writing with a thrift
and conciseness which critics attributed to the influence of Hemingway, another newcomer was in fact only reacting to the verbosity of
an expatriate American professor of literature.

The attempt to cross-catalogue the influences of writer upon writer
has little importance outside of keeping the literary archaeologist
busy. For the important influences to be brought to light perhaps a
psychoanalyst might be of help. From the artist's point of view (not
the archaeologist's) there are two types of influence. The artist may
copy or emulate the form of another and adapt his techniques, but
in dealing with translations we might well ask who it is that the
translator would emulate. The influence which reaches deeper, and
which may leave no telltale mound or even the slightest carbon-14
trace, is that influence which most inspires. And this may just as
easily be another art medium as a place or a person. But within his

own medium, a writer might be greatly influenced, say, by Faulkner's lectures on the success of failure and his idea—how very Oriental—of the inevitability of imperfection, and yet not be able to stomach Faulkner's writings. One might be inspired, say, by Selden Rodman's poetic biography of Lawrence of Arabia and strive to do what Rodman did—something comparable though not necessarily in the same form or style. The influences that count are those which contribute towards getting the "juice" (as Hemingway called it) to flowing. It may be other writers (a translator from the Chinese whom I know uses Erle Stanley Gardner), it may be a bottle (we all know so many), it may be a painting, a joint, a pipe, a needle, sharpening pencils, walking up a mountain, esoteric shadowboxing, dance drills, or the pressure of due bills. Any sort of personal mandala will do just so long as it gets the head spinning and produces the detachment and associations for freeing the juice. The really important influence may be rather the vector or nature of the action—active, meditative, monochrome, polychrome, uphill, pointed, circular, shadowy, real. To really plumb the effective influence would, I repeat, take psychoanalysis and a dissection thrown in. Any understanding this would give us of the artist or his art would not resemble that which he had hoped to convey and would be of as much use to us as his dead and dissected corpse.

And you question again, perhaps angrily, perhaps justly so, "How are we to appreciate it from our padded pedestal?" Just by looking at it and trying to appreciate it for what it is, or what it has pretensions of being, with no preconceived notions, no mental forewords. (One should never read a foreword or an introduction till one has finished the body of the book.) The why and the how and the wherefore of it all is far less important. It is enough that these writers wrote when they did of what they did.

Turning again to Lady Murasaki, one is, with her, still ". . . amazed at the advances which this art of fiction is now making," as Prince Genji exclaimed. "How do you suppose that our new writers come by this talent? It used to be thought that the authors of successful romances were merely particularly untruthful people whose imaginations had been stimulated by constantly inventing plausible lies. But that is clearly unfair. . . ."

"Perhaps," his companion answered, "only people who are themselves much occupied in practicing deception have the habit of thus dipping below the surface. I can assure you that for my part, when I read a story, I always accept it as an account of something that has really and actually happened."

Genji continued, "So you see, as a matter of fact I think far better of this art than I have led you to suppose. Even its practical value is immense. Without it what should we know of how people lived in the past . . . ? For history books . . . show us only one small corner of life; whereas these diaries and romances which I see piled around you contain, I am sure, the most minute information about all sorts of people's private affairs. . . . But I have a theory of my own . . . this art . . . does not simply consist in the author's telling a story about the adventures of some other person. On the contrary, it happens because the storyteller's own experience of men and things, whether for good or ill—not only what he has passed through himself, but even events which he has only witnessed or been told of—has moved him to an emotion so passionate that he can no longer keep it shut up in his heart. Again and again something in his own life or in that around him will seem to the writer so important that he cannot bear to let it pass into oblivion. There must never come a time, he feels, when men do not know about it."

Writing 950 years later in *Preview*, shortly after we had initiated the *Ukiyo* project, critic Mukai Hiroo noted: "The Japanese short story or novel can be a window through which the West may see Japan as it is. Though vicarious, the picture thus seen should be more true, poignant and intimate than the result of any fleeting visit to the country." Yet though this should be so, the picture presented is somehow superficial: as Takami Jun has said, Japan's was a hermit's literature for half a century.

The sudden surge towards Westernization began officially in 1867. A few short pieces in the old popular paperback style successfully dealt with the new modes—such as *The Beefeater* and *The Western Peep Show*, available in several translations. The new, even cheaper printing and the expanding literacy set off a deluge of pulp writing. The first Western-style success, which dates the official beginning of the new literature, was the novel *Ukigumo* (Floating Clouds), 1888. This followed close on the heels of *The Essence of the Novel* (the term used is the broader *sho-setsu*), 1885, a critical work which became the bible of writers for decades. *Essence* denounced the moralizing that had been the moving force behind fiction with any pretensions and called for esthetic realism. The discovery of the West permitted the Japanese artists to rediscover humanity. At about the same time many writers, pioneered by Mori Ogai, rediscovered the Self under the initial impetus of the German *Ich Roman,* "I Novel." But the development was singularly Japanese, with moral dialectics rejected with, again, such a vengeance that the naturalists became uncritical reporters: there were no crusaders. The *Ich Roman* turns more introspective in the extreme tradition of the ancient hermit notebooks, a fixation with one's own petty experiences and idle thoughts. Whereas the old hermit notebooks had been meditative views on life viewed with detachment, the Japanese "I Novel" became the product of navel-gazers who had forgotten why they were meditating. This was the main current of prewar Japanese literature, the most singularly Japanese, a natural product of the Thought Police State which developed, but also a great accessory to political development.

Japanese military victories against China and Russia at the turn of the century watered seeds of hope and encouraged the rise of a generation of Romantics. There was an Esthetic School, first given impetus by Oscar Wilde, Maeterlinck, Baudelaire, which was divorced from social problems, yet less decadent or hedonistic than the European *fin de siècle* writers. Natsume Soseki, a writer of Chinese poems and a student of English literature, returned from England with a British style of minimizing problems, with aloofness from privation the essence of his Leisure School. But the aloofness became confused by others with escapism. Natsume alone succeeded as the proverbial objective outsider, the man with the knowledge of experience used with the objectivity of detachment, and he wrote excellent satire (I Am a Cat) and penetrating analyses. A third romantic group exerted perhaps the greatest influence of any single band: the *Shirakaba-ha,* or White Birch School. This had a school-tie origin, consisting mostly of graduates of the Peers School. Their birthright entitled them to freedoms undreamed of by most other Japanese. They were idealists in the grand aristocratic tradition and they still maintain a faithful following among present-day "progressive" collegians for their fervor for human individuality and their concept of a humanity that transcends national and social categories. They are responsible for introducing much of the best of Western literature and art of the period.

Japanese literature of the generation that ended with the Great Earthquake of 1923 is dominated by this conflict between the naturalists and the romantic-idealists. But the situation of Japan and the world after World War I was intensely aggravated in Japan by the depression and the earthquake. The naturalists had tried to digest too much from the West and had turned into mere superficial imitators. It was not enough just to record. Romanticism was fatally dampened by hunger pangs. A new confrontation developed, that of the Proletarian Writers versus the Nationalists. It is a characteristic of Japan that foreign artists like Walt Whitman and Romain Rolland could be claimed as seminal influences for both the *fin de siècle* esthetes and the later proto-communists.

The breakdown of feudalism had provided the original impetus for the Proletarian Writers, but the end of World War I brought them to the fore. Within a short time they virtually monopolized the entire generation of artists. It was during this period that most of the professional writers represented in this collection arose. (Biographical sketches of all the contributors appear at the end of this volume.) Our selection is fairly representative of this conflict, though it was not consciously so planned. In brief, as in most of the industrialized nations, the various anarchist, socialist, and communist revolutionary ideas seized the imaginations of the intellectuals. Marxists soon took the lead, but other factions maintained sufficient strength to prevent them from taking control. The great depression brought the Nationalists to power and Japan started on her overseas "experiment." The successes of the semi-autonomous overseas army strengthened the militarists at home. Nationalism became the New Romanticism, old classics were disinterred for new worship, and often republished in heavily censored form. The Nationalists won out, not by greater literary showing, but by government control. Some of the better writers were caught in the middle, opposing both extremes. Most of those who published at all, and stayed out of jail, followed the old well-blazed path into personal hermitages. The strongest opposition was simply a withdrawal from writing. Others engaged in a harmless literature of decadence. Still others hacked out inane war pulp, descriptions of battles, evidencing neither perspiration nor inspiration.

The end of the war, in 1945, brought freedoms such as even the select White Birchers had not enjoyed, and this time for everyone. The American Occupation exerted a control over the press, but left the fictioneers to do as they wished. The hordes of political prisoners released from jail included writers who had been arrested for harboring suspicious thoughts (one writer was hauled off on account of "the thoughts evidenced by his facial expression" when an official car drove by, whereas in fact he had never noticed it; he was just annoyed that his wife was keeping him waiting). The hermitages had been bombed out, the hermits forced out into the remains of the world. Japanese literature started from scratch after 1945, but the writers were for the most part older men and women; a whole generation had been lost to literature.

The *Bibliography of Showa Literature* (from 1926 to the present), published in 1959, fourteen years after the war, lists approximately 750 authors alive at the end of the war, of whom those 30 years of age or less (under 44 at time of publication) number a mere 39.

The three stylistic groupings of postwar literature are the old "I Novel"; the Fiction of Manners, another old school but one that did not attain fame until now; and the *après guerre*. The division is not clear-cut. An author may be categorized by personal preference or by a slight predominance of one quality. The I-Novelist draws only upon the reality of his own life for material. In the Fiction of Manners the author goes outside himself, dealing with events of everyday life, somewhat like the American post-depression writers dealing with similar problems. The *après guerre* writers return to the individual and the suffering of man caused by the gap between himself and social conditions. But the "I Novel" is little more than a well-turned diary, and belongs more to the ancient diary tradition than to anything Western. The Fiction of Manners is of the stuff of the old picture scrolls, and rarely attains anything more than vignettes, and these are so much centered on one individual as to be as self-centered as the "I Novel." The *après guerre* rebel employs his version of Joycean stream-of-consciousness technique, Freudian psychoanalysis, illusion (when less successful, only delusion), and a return to the interior monologue of the medieval hermit tracts, all exaggerated, preciously oversensitive.

It is all best described by Edward Seidensticker as "the posings of the autobiographers . . . seldom is an idea allowed to trouble the works." It lacks the depth the Westerner expects of literature, just as the Japanese lack, as William Lederer points out, the ability to take (I would prefer "the concept of taking") a moral stand. There is emotional journalism of apology or complaint, but little literature of such grand-scale tragedies as Nanking or Hiroshima, or of the personal tragedy of the Kamikaze suicide troops, or the fate of an intellectual in a totalitarian society. Nakajima Kenzo points out that "the writers are afraid less of war itself than of the political repression which it brings," a fear that has become almost a conditioned reflex and which is as prevalent today as ever. This creates even in the "progressives" a nostalgia for the ancient national isolation from the world. But they have been thoroughly infected by the outside world and can never again successfully withdraw.

Modern Japanese literature was born of this mating of West with East. The seminal influences of the vigorous Occident cannot be underrated. The pioneers (and, as elsewhere, it seems that the great art was a product of the beginning) like Mori Ogai and Natsume Soseki were thoroughly acquainted with the best of the West in the original. (They were equally at home in the classics of Japan and China.) All the professionals are widely read in Western literature, whether they reject it or acclaim it. More important, the part played by translation into Japanese must be considered. A surprising number of professional writers are products of university departments of foreign literature (as are a great number of the journalists from whom the more recent "City News Room" school of shock literature has come), but this may only provide a gloss. Of the twenty authors interviewed "in depth" in Nakano Yoshio's *Writers of Today*, almost all admit to having been first awakened to literature by some translation from the West. Even the earliest attackers of "West worship," Kitamura Takubu and Ishikawa Takuboku, were not traditionalists harking back to the old isolation, but modernists demanding an absorption of the usable and the creation of something new and native. Of the modern greats, Kawabata Yasunari may be rare in that he was never "intoxicated by the West," was from his earliest conscious days fond of Japanese classics, but he is well acquainted with Occidental letters and makes good use of what his genius finds nourishing.

One still perceives the subtle shadows of Genji amidst the Western ferro-concrete and traffic jams. Characteristic of classical Japanese literature is *mono no aware,* considered an "untranslatable term" but approximately explainable as the sighing acknowledgment of the "Ahness of it all," of an awareness of the inherent sorrow of things, the appreciation of the implications of the moment of parting or of the fall of a leaf: but always applied to some moment or some outside object which might reflect a sparkle of enlightenment. At the hands of self-centered romantics in their hermitages it became a soft-sell melodramatic mournful awareness of the imagined futility of everything; any moment, and so all time, lost all power of projecting any implications. Now it is commonly evident only when the reader becomes aware of a moaning from the author: the cry of one drowning in the implications of the sinking of the old Floating World. This is not sarcastic criticism but simple recognition of the state of the intellectual as mirrored in the professional literature of Japan. It is a technique the Occidental author might well adapt. It is one that the boy in the mountain school and the dying Hiroshima housewife use with delicacy, effectively, because they are still capable of experiencing. In spite of the physical similarity to the West, of imitative styles and literary fads, of simulating the way of life of the characters, the reader of modern Japanese literature will, as Mukai Hiroo puts it, "find exoticism in the thought processes which the stories describe or reflect, will become aware of the Japanese mind's dislike of scientific and analytical methods, the lack of objectivity, the predominance of emotion" (which I would prefer to call sentimentality) "over reason, the tendency to look inward" (if with little of the Western novelist's inner searching or insight), "rather than outward, and the quest for beauty in simplicity."

The "quest for beauty in simplicity" may materialize in a tendency to merely oversimplify, or result in simple ambiguity. Japanese critics complain that translations of Japanese literature into English "make the meaning too clear." (However, letters to the editors of Japanese newspapers constantly complain of the ever-present ambiguity.) Other Japanese critics think that the literature, even the most avant-garde, is so rooted in traditional manners peculiar to Japan that it has been unable to rise above provincialism, and has not produced independent works of art endowed with the universal appeal of the Kabuki or Noh. Some feel that this rooting in peculiar mores makes it incomprehensible to anyone not already well versed in Japanese customs and history. The Western critic is not so exclusive or pessimistic: *The Pacific Spectator* feels that "Japan has the most prolific publishing business in the world"; Dr. Donald Keene, that "their literary output is among the world's best." I feel that whatever the volume or quality, what Prince Genji said a thousand years ago is still true, that Japanese history, any history, must remain incomprehensible to anyone who does not flesh out the bones of historical outlines with the living tissue of literature.

Stories have been selected for this volume which fill in a section of the picture scroll of the Floating World of Japan during that drifting decade after the end of the war. As editor of *View,* a *Life*-style monthly pictorial published in Tokyo, I had initiated a series of picture-and-text reports on typical, ordinary people—office girls, police patrolmen—the usual city-desk feature stuff, but in a broad context, with an over-all book in mind. All of my associates were Japanese, yet the stories lacked depth, veracity. We hunted through the Japanese magazines to see how they handled similar situations. I was no more satisfied. Then I rediscovered the *Genji Monogatari* dialogue on the essence of the novel which some graduate-school lecturer had referred to in passing and which I had jotted down in shorthand in my notes. Perhaps oddly, the lecturer was an Egyptian, the noted Arab littérateur, translator, and exile, Ahmed Zaky Abushady, my professor of Arabic at the Asia Institute, who managed to instill in his students a sympathetic understanding, almost empathy, for the recent history of the Middle East through a selection of literature. It was my good fortune that the advisory editor to *View* at that time was Charles Cooke, an O. Henry Award short-story writer whose unselfish advice was invaluable. The staff was put to work scouting suitable material, and out of this my principal collaborators emerged, Grace Suzuki and Momoi Makoto. In May 1952 I took over simultaneous editorship of the sister magazine *Preview* and the first test stories appeared in its pages. When I left the company and formed my own *Orient Digests,* by common consent the project moved with me. Several stories appeared in this magazine, the Japan PEN Club gave a lunch to discuss the planned book, lent their generous cooperation, and eleven stories were published in book form for Japan-Korea circulation under this same title, *Ukiyo,* ten of which are reprinted here.

There was no attempt to represent literary trends or representative writers. Indeed, at about the same time the PEN Club had been called upon to nominate writers and stories for a UNESCO anthology, of which the recent *Modern Japanese Short Stories,* edited by Ivan Morris, is the product. The first thin Orient edition of *Ukiyo* presented a picture of Japan that was far from complete, but the omissions were not ours. They were a product of the hermit tradition and the "posings of the autobiographers." No Japanese novelists had been leading militarists, nor had any writers yet risen out of the ranks of the war children. And it seemed no "autobiographer" was going to sit down and do a deep character analysis of another person, especially a former persecutor, in order to write a biographical novel.

Many of the short stories and parts of novels in this collection are barely disguised autobiography. They are fiction only in technique, and certainly far less fictitious than much avowedly factual memoirs. At *Preview* I had been in charge of another project, the editing and rewriting of Colonel Tsuji Masanobu's and convicted war criminal Kodama Yoshio's reminiscences of the war and the immediate aftermath. These had appeared earlier in garbled but nonetheless valuable translations, and my new editions (from which this selection comes) were never issued. At *Orient Digests* we continued this idea, Momoi and I, by translating and publishing selections of this military nonfiction, which was at the time the most popular product of the Japanese magazines, intending to show the Japanese view of the war. From this project comes the Yokoi selection.

Added since, to fill some still-felt lacunae, have been the amateur diaries, which today are still as much a part of the literature as they were in Genji's time.

NOTES: All fully Japanese names appear in the Japanese manner, Family name first, personal name last. All vowels are pronounced as in Italian (far, fit, true, fed, so), but diacritical marks to indicate long vowels have been eliminated; *j* as in English usage, *g* always hard, no syllable accented.

IMPERIAL RESCRIPT

To Our Good and Loyal Subjects:

After pondering deeply the general trend of the world and the actual conditions obtaining in Our Empire today, We have decided to effect a settlement of the present situation by resorting to an extraordinary measure.

We have ordered Our Government to inform the Governments of the United States, Great Britain, China, and the Soviet Union that Our Empire accepts the provisions of their Joint Declaration.

To strive for the common prosperity and happiness of all nations as well as the security and well-being of Our subjects is the solemn obligation which has been handed down by Our Imperial Ancestors, and which We lay close to Our heart. Indeed, We declared war on America and Britain out of Our sincere desire to ensure the self-preservation of Japan and the stabilization of East Asia, it being far from Our thought either to infringe upon the sovereignty of other nations or to embark upon territorial aggrandizement. But now the war has lasted for nearly four years. Despite the best that has been done by everyone—the gallant fighting of the military and naval forces, the diligence and assiduity of Our servants of the State and the devoted service of Our one hundred million people—the military situation has developed to Japan's disadvantage, while the general trends of the world have all turned against her interest. Moreover, the enemy has begun to employ a new and most cruel bomb, the power of which to do damage is indeed incalculable, and which has already taken many innocent lives. Should We continue to fight, it not only would result in an ultimate collapse and obliteration of the Japanese nation, but would also lead to the total extinction of human civilization. Such being the case, how are We to save the millions of Our subjects; or to atone for Our actions before the hallowed spirits of Our Imperial Ancestors? This is the reason why We have ordered the acceptance of the provisions of the Joint Declaration of the Powers.

We cannot but express the deepest sense of regret to our Allied nations of East Asia, who have consistently cooperated with the Empire towards the emancipation of East Asia. The thought of those officers and men as well as others who have fallen in the fields of battle, those who died at their posts of duty, or those who met with untimely death and all their bereaved families, pains Our heart night and day. The welfare of the wounded and the suffering, and of those who have lost their homes and livelihood, are the objects of Our profound solicitude. The hardships and suffering to which Our nation is to be subjected hereafter will certainly be great. We are keenly aware of the innermost feelings of all ye, Our subjects. However, it is according to the dictate of time and fate that We have resolved to pave the way for a grand peace for all the generations to come by enduring the unendurable and suffering what is insufferable.

Having been able to safeguard and maintain the structure of the Imperial State, We are always with ye, Our good and loyal subjects, relying upon your sincerity and integrity. Beware most strictly of any outbursts of emotion which may engender needless complication, or any fraternal contention and strife which may create confusion, lead ye astray, and cause ye to lose the confidence of the world. Let the entire nation continue as one family from generation to generation, ever firm in its faith of the imperishability of its divine land, and mindful of its heavy burden of responsibilities, and the long road before it. Devote all your strength to the construction of the future. Cultivate the ways of rectitude; foster nobility of spirit; and work with resolution so as ye may enhance the innate glory of the Imperial State and keep pace with the progress of the world.

(Imperial Sign Manual)

(Imperial Seal)

The 14th day of the 8th month
of the 20th year of Showa

—*translated from* The Nippon Times, *August 15, 1945*

THREE UNFORGETTABLE LETTERS

by Taguchi Shu

ON DECEMBER 7, 1941, when the report was flashed over the air that Japan had made a sudden attack on Pearl Harbor, I was engaging in jovial conversation with intimate American friends in my apartment in New York City. The report came like a bolt from the blue and suddenly made these dear friends enemies and me an enemy of theirs, and I could not grasp the fantastic idea at all. Rather the fateful war that had then been set into motion appeared to me like an affair involving entirely distant worlds, with no relation to me.

A short time afterwards I was placed under detention at Ellis Island as an enemy national. Whether the war between my country and America had ever occurred to me as an actuality or not, when at last I found myself incarcerated, it dawned upon me like a blast of icy wind that my status now was that of an enemy national. With this realization, I was overcome by indescribable feelings of loneliness, insecurity, and despair.

There at Ellis Island more than two hundred of my fellow countrymen were detained with me. Each had his own world of worries, but over all there hovered demoralizing insecurity. As for me, isolated as I was from the outer world, it was wretchedness itself to gaze out of windows covered with meshed steel wires from morning to night, to see before my very eyes the massive and towering figure of Manhattan in whose gay streets I had spent so many pleasurable moments. More than by a feeling of uncertainty and

1

hopelessness, I was crushed by the reality of my unhappy isolation from the world I loved so dearly.

It was at such a time that a letter came—a letter that gave me heart and made my feelings soar:

My Dear Shu:

After some time and effort, I have at last ascertained that it was not illegal to write letters to an enemy national and I now hasten to write this. My purpose of course is to try to give you whatever spiritual comfort I can, for your sudden change of environment and the sudden shock may have thrown you into an abyss of despair, and also to show you that your American friends are not merely fair-weather friends. Friendship should not be a relationship maintained only in fair weather. People need an umbrella only when it rains. If friendship means merely going on picnics or to the movies together, the word "friend" is just a word and no more. And if anybody needed a friend now you need one the most. Even if the whole world should become one's enemy and one is overcome with discouragement and despair, I know by experience that the mere knowledge that one has a friend—even only one—whose heart is true, supplies one with strength, courage, and hope.

I believe without one iota of doubt that the censor who will check this letter and the Americans who surround you daily are people who have the right concept and consciousness of human equality, justice, and freedom, and are people who will not look upon the individual with prejudice. It is because of this that I believe they will not prevent a letter written with a sincere motive from reaching you.

From the very first, I have never considered it irregular or unlawful for one to entertain friendly affections for another even if their respective countries are at war with each other. The ability to draw a clear line of distinction between individual sentiments and racial prejudice and national movements—that is the virtue and wisdom of American democracy. I have never, ever, doubted this fact.

I have so little spare time now. Even if I were at complete liberty to write to you my conscience does not permit me to use the office typewriter during office hours. . . . It is a joy to know and to feel that by many small efforts I am contributing in some way to the cause of my country. Such being the case, I do not have much time.

It is one's human obligation to write letters and to comfort a friend in unhappy circumstances.

For me, there is no greater joy than to write to you. And my conscience is clear. To enjoy life and help others to enjoy it without harming anyone—herein lies the whole of morality. These words which I read in some book at some time and left a deep impression on me have just occurred to me. If this humble letter of mine could give you some comfort and encouragement, nothing would bring me greater joy.

There are moments when a person feels utterly powerless. Especially now in a world which moves with such force as to be beyond our power to resist. It is difficult to foresee one's fate. But please do not ever lose hope. When one discovers how powerless he is in the environment in which he lives, it is said that he becomes truly aware of the meaning of Truth. It is seldom that those of us who are apt to be bewildered by social phenomena in our ordinary everyday life are favored with such opportunities for meditation.

If we think of your present circumstances in such a light, we can say that you are not wasting time. Do not be disheartened and please continue to keep your spirits high and your courage unconquerable. It is my fervent prayer that you will have all the happiness possible under the present conditions.

Your American friend,

X

Thereafter, during a long period of detention, I received several such letters, full of friendly affection and inspiration. I need not say how these letters encouraged, taught, and enriched my daily life.

After seven months of life under detention at Ellis Island, in Virginia, and finally in West Virginia, arrangements were completed for our repatriation.

Those who had families in Japan and felt concern for them were overjoyed. But I was saddened by the thought that my repatriation would mean that these letters which had been the pillars of my strength might cease coming to me—forever. The departure of the repatriation ship was probably kept secret, for it was never reported in the papers. And so it pained me to think that my friend, not knowing that I had left, would keep on writing to me only to get letters back undelivered.

The time for embarkation came—a hot day in June. Across Manhattan on the New Jersey side was the Swedish liner, the *Gripsholm*, which was to take us as far as Lourenço Marques, Mozambique, in southern Africa. We boarded her on June 11, many of my fellow countrymen breathing a deep sigh as they looked at towering Manhattan for what might be the last time. Reluctant to leave the country where they had been born and brought up, many of the teen-agers had tears in their eyes as they trod up the gangplank.

After the baggage inspection, I was escorted by a steward to my stateroom. No sooner had I entered it than a pink-faced, jovial man came in. He was the purser. "You're Mr. Taguchi, aren't you?" he asked. "Have you seen the letter under the pillow? I'm sorry, but because of censorship regulations we had to see it before you. You're a very fortunate man, I can tell you, to have such a good friend."

I immediately rushed to my cot, lifted the pillow, and picked up the letter. It said:

My Dear Shu:

In the hope that this note will be delivered to you through the kindness of the purser, I am taking this opportunity to send you a few words of farewell. Now that you are about to leave for your country, I want you to go with the knowledge that your friends in America are ceaselessly praying for your happiness and our reunion, which we hope will not be too far away.

When you return to your country, a new life and a completely different environment will no doubt meet you. My present concern is that the thought conveyed to you through my letters might bring or cause you unhappiness, and I fevently pray that my fears are unfounded. Until the day this sad and awful war ends, I intend to devote my heart and soul to the cause of my country. But I will continue to pray from the bottom of my heart for your happiness. When this war has ended and when mankind may again enjoy the blessings of peace and freedom, we shall be able to resume our friendship.

Whatever fate may unfold, I assure you that you will always be in my heart. Remember always, please, that your friendship and your trust have greatly enriched my life and my thoughts.